Jimmy Mars

ALIEN

in my belly button

Illustrated by Chris Garbutt

EGMONT

EGMONT

 With special thanks to
Barry Hutchison

Alien in my belly button
First published in Great Britain 2012
by Egmont UK Limited
239 Kensington High Street
London W8 6SA

Text copyright © 2012 Hothouse Fiction
Illustrations copyright © 2012 Chris Garbutt
All rights reserved.

The moral rights of the author and illustrator have been asserted

ISBN 978 1 4052 5506 6

1 3 5 7 9 10 8 6 4 2

www.egmont.co.uk

A CIP catalogue record for this title is available from the British Library

Printed and bound by CPI Group (UK) Ltd, Croydon, CR0 4YY

47421/1

EGMONT LUCKY COIN

Our story began over a century ago, when seventeen-year-old Egmont Harald Petersen found a coin in the street.

He was on his way to buy a flyswatter, a small hand-operated printing machine that he then set up in his tiny apartment.

The coin brought him such good luck that today Egmont has offices in over 30 countries around the world. And that lucky coin is still kept at the company's head offices in Denmark.

CONTENTS

CHAPTER ONE

A VERY CLOSE ENCOUNTER

Pete Perkins was right in the middle of his favourite dream: the one where he zoomed around a big rollercoaster made of jelly. He zipped this way and that, munching on his raspberry-flavoured seat when . . .

VROOM!

'WAAAAAAGH!'

With a yelp, Pete sat straight up in bed. His foot was itchy. No, not just itchy. He'd felt itchy before. This was worse – much worse. It was a burning, scratchy feeling, as if tiny insects with spiky shoes were having a party between his toes. Throwing back his covers, Pete shoved a finger down between his big toe and the one beside it and rubbed hard.

2

When he was sure the prickliness had gone, Pete lay back on his pillow, trying to ignore the cheesy smell from his finger. Across the room in the other bed, his little brother, Ollie, carried on snoring.

'What was that about?' muttered Pete. He'd never felt an itch that bad before, and he hoped he'd never feel one again.

ZOOOM!

With a bright flash, a red light shot in through the bedroom window, rocketed across the room and slammed into Pete's tummy.

'**AARGH!**' he cried. It was so sore it made his eyes water – even more than the time he'd eaten six of his mum's rock cakes for a dare and hadn't been able to go to the loo for a week.

What on Earth could it be?

Pete peered down and his eyes went wide with surprise. A tiny person was climbing out of his belly button!

The figure was smaller than Pete's little finger. It was wearing a shiny space-suit with black boots and a round helmet that looked like a goldfish bowl. It pulled itself out of Pete's belly button and up on to his stomach, and took off its helmet.

'Greetings,' it said, wiping sweat off

its bright green face. 'Sorry about that, but . . . **FLAMPERING PUFFLEFARTS!** You're huge!'

'No I am not!' spluttered Pete. 'You're *teeny*.'

'Oi! No need to get personal,' the figure said sniffily. 'Just cos I crash-landed in your belly button from outer space.'

'What?' Pete gasped. 'Did you just say you're from *space*?'

The tiny being brought out a little machine that looked like a calculator and pointed it at Pete. It made a whirring noise. 'Wowzers,' he said. 'You humans are meant to be the smartest creatures on this planet . . . slightly more clever than something called a monkey.' The small stranger shook the device and put it back in his pocket. 'Maybe it's broken.'

'Wait.' Pete frowned. 'So you're . . .

you're an actual *alien*?'

'I suppose. To you anyway. You're an alien to me. I'm Binko of the Planet Pok. **ZANPOOP!** Or "pleased to meet you" as you would say!' The alien put two fingers up his nose and then flicked them up into the air in a funny salute. Pete didn't want to seem rude so he copied Binko, finding a nice squidgy bogey in his left nostril.

'Planet Pok? Never heard of it,' he

8

muttered, wiping his snotty finger on his pyjama bottoms. He was starting to think he might still be dreaming.

'That doesn't mean it's not real,' replied Binko. 'I mean, I bet you've never heard of a moonswaggling snogpong either, have you?'

'A *what?*'

'A moonswaggling snogpong . . . It's an ickimal,' said Binko. 'Sort of like your Earth animals, only . . .'

'Ickier?' Pete asked.

'Exactly!' cried the alien. 'Don't suppose you've seen any of them around, have you?'

'Err, no, I don't think so. The only icky thing in this room is *him*,' said Pete, pointing at Ollie, who was snorting and dribbling in his sleep.

'I see what you mean. That *is* pretty disgusting,' said Binko, nodding. 'Well, if you do see any –'

Suddenly, Binko was interrupted by the screech of an alarm from somewhere inside his spacesuit.

'What is it?' Pete hissed. 'What's wrong?'

'It's an ickimal,' Binko whispered, pressing buttons on the arm of his suit. 'And it's somewhere nearby!'

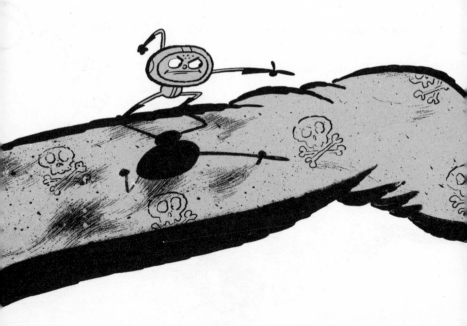

Pete sucked his breath in hard. 'Is it dangerous?'

'Yep. Dangerous and disgusting,' said Binko. 'It must be . . . *A-ha*!'

Binko scurried down Pete's leg, leaping over the wrinkles in his pyjamas like an Olympic hurdles champion.

He'd just done a perfect double flip when Pete noticed he was chasing something. Before Pete could move, the thing plunged head-first into the gap between his toes, closely followed by Binko.

The itching came back worse than ever. It felt like someone was tickling his foot with a cheese grater. Pete pulled his toes apart and for the second time that morning, he couldn't believe his eyes.

Wrestling with Binko was a creature the size of a peanut with long, drooping arms and sharp, prickly black hairs covering its entire body!

The hairy little beast looked up at Pete and opened its mouth to reveal two rows of shark-like teeth. With a yelp, Pete kicked out with his foot, sending Binko and the strange creature flying.

Pete jumped up and looked around

the room in a panic.

'Hello?' he whispered. 'Binko? Where are you?'

'Erm, I don't know,' said Binko's tiny voice. 'But it's dark and smells of wee.'

Aha, Pete thought. *I bet I know where he is*. He crept over to the pile of washing at the bottom of Ollie's bed. Lying inside a pair of Ollie's dirty pants was Binko.

Pete gently plucked him out

17

and sat him on the palm of his hand. 'Are you OK?' he asked.

'I'm fine,' said Binko. 'But where's the chimple?'

'The what?'

'The chimple!' said Binko again. 'The ickimal! The hairy thing with the teeth! Where did it go?'

Pete looked all around. At first he couldn't see anything. Then he spotted the

weird creature scurrying across the carpet
like a hairy spider.

'There it goes!' Pete said, pointing.

But the chimple was already at the
bedroom door. It slipped underneath with
a gurgling laugh and disappeared.

'We have to catch it,' Binko told him. The alien's tiny face suddenly looked very serious. 'If we don't, every person on this planet is in terrible danger!'

'Err, what do you mean "terrible danger"?' Pete demanded. 'It's not going to . . .' he gulped, '*kill* anyone, is it?'

'Worse,' replied Binko. 'It's going to make their feet really, really itchy!'

Pete peered down at the tiny alien

and blinked. 'Is that all?'

'Chimples burrow down deep under your toenails and wriggle around so that the spiky hairs on their bodies stick them tightly in place. That's what causes the itching. Then they start licking, slurping and sucking on all the dirty, mouldy old toe cheese that grows there.'

'I felt it a few minutes ago,' Pete said, nodding. 'It was bad.'

'And that was when it was probably just sniffing about trying to find something to eat – nothing compared to how it feels when a chimple's actually scoffing all your toe cheese. You can go stark raving bonkers from the itching. Some purgumps on Pok have sawn off their own feet just to make it stop!'

'Really?' gasped Pete.

'Yes!' Binko exclaimed. 'But then

purgumps do have five thousand feet, so it doesn't matter that much.'

The alien pulled himself up to his full height – which wasn't very high at all – and looked Pete in the eye. 'You have to help me. You have to help me stop the chimple!'

CHAPTER TWO
BREAKFAST TIME

Pete sat down on his bed, with Binko balanced on his hand. Sunlight had begun to push in through the window.

'I still don't understand,' Pete said. 'How did the chimple get here?'

Binko rubbed his hands together nervously. 'Um . . . well, you see . . . it's sort of . . . I mean, you might say . . .'

'It's your fault, isn't it?' Pete asked.

Binko nodded. 'Yes.' He sighed sadly. 'My mum and dad run an ickimal zoo on Pok. I sort of accidentally let some of the ickimals out and they escaped into space on the back of a Pokian rubbish ship.'

'Wow. Bet your parents were angry,' Pete said.

'They will be,' Binko replied, 'if they ever find out. They're off on a cruise around the galaxy at the moment. I've tracked the ickimals here, and if I can catch them all before mum and dad get back, they don't ever need to know what happened.'

'But why did the ickimals come to Earth?' Pete asked.

'Ickimals like to live in the most disgusting places they can find, so I bet they jumped ship when they saw Earth,' explained Binko. 'It's the ickiest planet in the galaxy – everybody knows that – and your garden shows up as a grot hot-spot.'

'That must be because of Grandpa

Bob,' said Pete. 'We call him G-Bob for short. He lives in the shed.'

'Why do you make him live in the shed?' Binko sounded confused.

'We don't. He likes it out there,' Pete replied. 'I think it's because it doesn't have a bathroom. He *hates* taking baths.'

'Boys. Yoo hoo, wakey wakey!' sang a voice from downstairs. 'Time to get up!'

Across the room, Ollie sat straight up in bed.

'Morning, Ollie.' Pete smiled, cupping his fingers to hide Binko.

'Moaning Pit!' shouted Ollie. He stuck out his tongue at his big brother and marched out of the room.

'What did he say?' asked Binko, popping his head up through a gap in Pete's fingers.

'He *meant* to say, "Morning, Pete",' explained Pete, 'but he can't speak very well yet. He's only two.'

'Hmmm, I see,' said Binko. 'So, back to business. I need someone very talented, brave and cleverer than an oongaloid warper to help me catch the ickimals.'

Pete smiled.

'I don't suppose you know anyone like that, do you?' Binko continued.

Pete's smile turned to a frown, and the little alien burst out laughing. 'Just kidding! Will *you* help?'

'OK, but we have to be careful. If anyone else sees you, they'll go mad!'

'No problem!' Binko grinned and Pete felt a sudden warmth on his hand as two

tiny bursts of flame shot from a jet-pack on Binko's spacesuit. The little alien flew up through the air and circled Pete's head a few times.

'Wow!' gasped Pete, who was spinning around trying to keep his eye on the alien. 'I wish I had one of those!'

Binko chuckled. With a quick double backflip, he landed neatly on the top of Pete's ear.

'I can hide in your hair,' he said. 'Can you hear me?'

'Yep.' Pete nodded.

'Watch it!' yelped Binko. 'You nearly shook me off.'

'Oops! Sorry,' Pete said, grinning cheekily.

'By the way,' said the alien, 'do you know you have dandruff?'

Pete sighed and got to his feet. Binko

was trouble. But he sort of liked him. Things were definitely more interesting with him around.

'We'd better go down for breakfast,' Pete muttered to Binko as he walked down the stairs and headed into the kitchen.

'Oh zooper,' Binko said in Pete's ear. 'I'm starving!'

'Well, you won't be when you see my mum's cooking,' Pete whispered glumly.

'But whatever happens make sure you keep out of sight!'

At the kitchen table, Pete stared at the bowl Willow had put in his usual place. Willow was Pete and Ollie's mum.

'What's this?' Pete asked suspiciously while Ollie sat across the table, poking at his own bowl with a plastic spoon. 'It's porridge, of course,' Willow said with a beaming smile.

'What's the pink stuff?' Pete asked.

'Rose petals.'

Pete looked up at his mum in horror. '*Rose petals?*'

'Told you this planet was disgusting,' whispered Binko, somewhere in Pete's hair.

'They're full of solar energy,' Willow explained. 'I read about it in a magazine. Eating a rose petal is like taking a bite of the sun itself!'

'I wouldn't recommend biting a sun,'
said Binko quietly. 'It took months for my
lips to grow back last time.'

'Can't we just have Choco-Flakes?' Pete asked.

'Choggo-Fakes! Mmmmm! Choggo-Fakes!' agreed Ollie loudly, banging his chubby fists on the table.

'Of course you can, Poppy-Kitten.' Willow smiled and pressed Pete gently on the end of his nose. 'Or you *could*, if I hadn't used them last night.'

'You can't have eaten them *all*,' said

Pete. Even *he* couldn't eat a whole box.

'I didn't *eat* them, my little Lemon-Flower,' replied Willow. 'I *used* them. To make this.' She held up her wrist, proudly displaying a brown bracelet made of crunchy flakes of cereal held together with string. 'It's a breakfast bracelet. Whenever I'm hungry, I can just take a nibble.'

Pete wasn't sure what to say. In the end, Binko said it for him.

'Your mum's loopier than a loogal.'

Willow turned back to the sink and Pete looked over at Ollie who was now picking his nose with the end of his spoon, teasing out yellowy globs of snot and flicking them across the room at his mum's back.

Pete was watching the snot build up on Willow's homemade cardigan when the back door swung open with a bang.

A huge, towering figure stood in the doorway, glaring into the kitchen. It was a man with dirty, food-spattered clothes and a long, bushy beard that looked like some- one had hidden a whole plate of dinner in it. A foul smell wafted through the door.

'That's G-Bob!' Pete whispered.

'He *stinks*!' spluttered Binko into Pete's ear.

As G-Bob shuffled into the kitchen,

a scruffy ball of fur darted through his legs with an angry hiss. It was Pete's one-eyed cat, Scar-face.

'Filthy little brute,' growled G-Bob, wiping his nose on his sleeve. 'One of these days I'll squish it flat.' G-Bob's bare feet slapped across the floor, leaving grimy footprints as he walked over to the table.

'Morning, G-Bob,' said Pete.

'Gee Bob! Gee Bob! Gee Bob!' yelled

Ollie, rocking in his high chair, blowing delighted spit bubbles and knocking the salt cellar over. Pete picked it up – and grinned. He had an idea.

'Do you play practical jokes on Pok?' he whispered to Binko as quietly as he could.

'Oh yes!' laughed Binko. 'Once I stuck someone's bomtom to a purple zark. You should have seen his face!'

'I have no idea what that means,' said Pete. 'But watch this.'

Pete quickly emptied the salt into a neat pile on the table. Snatching up the sugar bowl, he poured its contents into the empty salt cellar, then swept the salt into the sugar bowl. The whole thing took less than five seconds.

G-Bob had sat down and was now staring at the food in front of him. 'What's this pink stuff?' he asked, peering down at his porridge.

'Rose petals,' explained Pete.

'Gah!' snorted G-Bob. He dug a dirty hand in the porridge, pulled the petals out in one big, gloopy fistful and dropped the mush on the table with a *splat*. Wiping his hand on his stained shirt, G-Bob reached for the sugar bowl and sprinkled a big helping over what was left of his porridge.

From near his ear, Pete heard Binko giggle excitedly. Pete fought back a snigger of his own as G-Bob lifted his spoon and scooped up some of the lumpy sludge. G-Bob opened his mouth, showing a set of blackened teeth with half of last night's dinner still stuck in them. He shovelled the food in, making a loud slurping noise.

Suddenly his cheeks puffed out and his eyes boggled.

'BlEEEEEE EEURGH!'

he spluttered, spitting the mouthful into the bowl. 'That's *disgustin'*! Tastes like some fish have done a salty wee in it.'

PTOOEY!

48

'*Dee*-gustin'!' agreed Ollie. He tried to spit out his own porridge, but in his excitement he forgot to open his mouth. Instead a snotty goo came out through his nose and shot on to the table, slopping all over the rose petals.

SNOT!

'Zooper trick, Pete!' Binko giggled in his ear.

Pete was trying not to laugh when suddenly a loud noise came from under the table. It sounded like the whistle of a boiling kettle. Pete looked down to see what was going on and saw Scar-face hissing dangerously.

His fur was standing on end like he'd been electrocuted and his one eye was bulging madly. A tiny screeching sound went off right by Pete's ear. Binko's ickimal alarm!

'Uh-oh!' Binko whispered urgently. 'It's here! The chimple is here!'

CHAPTER THREE
HUNT THE CHIMPLE

'Whoops!' said Pete, deliberately dropping his spoon on to the floor. 'I'd better pick that up.'

He ducked down under the table. Scar-face looked up at him and made another horrible, strangled hissing noise.

'There's definitely something down here,' Pete whispered to Binko. 'Scar-face is being even weirder than usual. So where's the chimple?'

'**FLAMPERING PUFFLEFARTS,** where do you think?' Binko said. 'On someone's foot!'

Pete stared at the three pairs of bare feet in front of him.

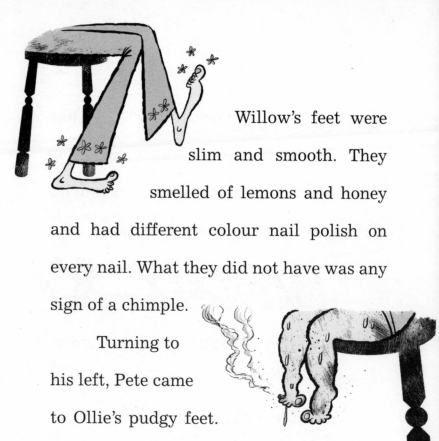

Willow's feet were slim and smooth. They smelled of lemons and honey and had different colour nail polish on every nail. What they did not have was any sign of a chimple.

Turning to his left, Pete came to Ollie's pudgy feet. One was half-coated in porridge.

The other was sticky with what looked like mashed banana. Pete couldn't see anything moving about on them, but he leaned in for a closer look, just to make sure.

Ollie swung both feet up, catching Pete on the chin.

'Ow!' Pete yelped, leaping back.

'*Ouch!*' He yelped again as his head

smacked against the underside of the table.

'**wAAAGH!**' cried Binko, losing

his grip and almost slipping off Pete's ear.

Willow's voice floated down from above the table. 'Petey? Are you OK down there, Bran-Muffin?'

'Oh, just looking for my spoon,' lied Pete, rubbing his head.

Ollie's feet were too dangerous to study up close. Besides, Pete couldn't see any sign of the chimple. That left only one place to check . . .

Pete turned and found himself face-to-foot with G-Bob. His eyes began to water at the smell. G-Bob's feet stank like the juice at the bottom of a fifty-year-old dustbin. The soles were caked with mud, the tops were thick with yellow mould and hanging from one heel was something that looked like dog droppings. But most importantly,

grinning up from behind G-Bob's stinky,

hairy toes, was the chimple!

'Wish me luck,' cried Binko, firing up

his jet-pack and rocketing to G-Bob's foot.

The chimple darted into the deep, dark gap between two of G-Bob's toes.

'YoWEEEEE!'

shouted G-Bob, yanking his foot up suddenly. He glared under the table at Pete. 'What the flamin' 'eck are you doing to my foot?'

'N-n-nothing,' replied Pete. 'It was, err, Scar-face.'

'Is everything OK?' asked Willow, placing a soothing hand on to G-Bob's shoulder.

'Itchy!' G-Bob wailed, grabbing at his foot. 'Itchy, itchy, *itchy*!'

'Eechee! Eechee! Eecheeee!' echoed Ollie.

Pete gasped as G-Bob's fat finger stabbed down between his toes, only just missing Binko, who had to swing out of the way on one of G-Bob's greasy toe hairs. As the finger scratched back and forth, huge chunks of flaky skin scattered all over the kitchen like bits of grated cheese. And in the middle of it all scurried the chimple, running down G-Bob's big toe.

'Quick! Stop it!' yelled Binko, but it was too late. With a toothy cackle, the chimple darted into the dark, squidgy gap beneath G-Bob's big toenail . . .

CHAPTER FOUR

G-BOB'S WORST NIGHTMARE

'YOWBLEDOO!' howled G-Bob, leaping up off his chair, his beard standing on end in shock.

'What's the matter?' asked Willow.

'WHOOBKAK!' G-Bob shrieked,

hopping and dancing madly all around the kitchen. The itching was so bad now that he couldn't even speak properly.

'GUMMAGUMMAGUMMAGUMMA!'

'Hurpaloo!' giggled Ollie, joining in G-Bob's new game. 'Bullamumbellybum!'

Pete tried to see if Binko was still holding on to G-Bob's toe hairs, but he couldn't get close enough to tell.

'Binko?' Pete hissed, his voice low.

'Binko, where are you?'

'Here I am,' panted Binko, right in Pete's ear, nearly making him jump out of his skin. '**FLAMPERING PUFFLEFARTS**, there was no way I was going under *there*. I'd rather clean out a waxer's cage!'

With another howl, G-Bob snatched up his porridge spoon and began digging beneath his big toenail.

'So what do we do now?' Pete whispered.

Binko giggled as G-Bob spun wildly and bumped into the fruit bowl, sending plums and peaches splattering everywhere.

'Maybe we should just watch this for a while,' he laughed.

'He's going to wreck the place!' Pete replied with a grin.

G-Bob suddenly slipped up on a squashed plum and fell on his back with a

Even lying on the floor, G-Bob was still scraping away at his toenail. With each stab of the spoon, large nuggets of toe cheese went soaring across the kitchen.

Pete ducked one of the crusty, smelly

yellow lumps only to see it land with a loud *plop* in his bowl of porridge.

'Stop thrashing about. Find your *inner peace*,' Willow suggested. She closed her eyes and tried to show G-Bob how. '*Ommmm,*' she chanted. '*Ommmm!*'

'Bummmm,' Ollie yelled in response. '*Buuuuummmmm!*'

'Flippin 'ek, shut yer cake holes the lot of you!' roared G-Bob, his face now twitching in agony. 'I'm SO itchy!'

Willow looked hurt. 'No need to be a grumpy bunny. There's only one thing for it. I'm running you a lovely bath.'

Pete gasped. G-Bob almost choked on his beard. Even Ollie, who had been flicking porridge at the walls and screeching for the past ten seconds, fell silent.

G-Bob's face went red. Then purple. G-Bob *never* took baths.

He opened his mouth, tipped back

his head and gave a bellow that made the windows rattle.

He tried to scramble out of the door, but he couldn't walk and scratch his foot as the same time, so he fell over again. '**AAAAARRRGH!**' he screamed. '**OWOWOWOWOW!** It's gettin' WORSE!'

Willow bent down and put a hand on G-Bob's shoulder. 'Are you sure you don't want that bath, Mr Itchy? It might help.'

'OK,' G-Bob whispered, his face paling with fear. 'I'll do it. I'll do anythin'! Just make the itching stop!'

Willow slipped out of the kitchen and skipped up the stairs.

Pete looked at G-Bob, trying to remember if he'd ever seen him clean. Ollie had given up decorating the kitchen with porridge and was now quietly rubbing it into his hair instead. The gloop dribbled down his face and dripped off his chin. He looked like Willow when she used one of her homemade beauty facemasks.

'D'you think the chimple's still in there?' asked Pete quietly.

'Yes,' replied Binko. 'And your mum's right – the bath will flush it out. Chimples hate water. We'll have to be ready in case it makes a break for it.'

Pete nodded. He still couldn't quite believe that G-Bob was actually going to take a bath.

'Up you come then, G-Bob!' trilled Willow.

With a moan, G-Bob hobbled up the stairs, closely followed by Pete.

'Ta-daaa!' beamed Willow, gesturing towards the bathtub. Gallons of water poured down into it, and there were clouds of sweet-smelling steam billowing out into the hallway.

'Wha– what is *that*?' demanded G-Bob, hopping backwards. 'What's that *stuff*?'

'That's water,' Willow told him. '*Water*. We use it to get clean.'

'Not that – *that*,' G-Bob growled, stabbing a finger towards the edge of the steaming bath.

'Oh, those. Just a few scented candles,' Willow explained.

'And lots of girly bubble bath!' Pete sniggered. Binko laughed too, peeking out through Pete's hair. Even Ollie had crawled up the stairs to watch the show.

The air was filled with the clean smells of apple and mint. Pete wished he could see G-Bob's face, but he had his back to them.

'Will he do it?' Binko whispered.

'Not a chance,' Pete replied.

'But the itching will be driving him crazy!' said Binko.

'The thought of getting in that bath will be worse still,' replied Pete. 'Trust me.'

'I bet you forty pakloons he gets in the bath,' offered Binko.

Pete frowned. 'What's a pakloon? Is it money on Planet Pok?'

'No. It's an animal like a goat with a budgie's face,' Binko explained.

'Um . . . no, I won't bother then,' replied Pete.

'Suit yourself.' Binko shrugged. 'All the more for me.'

'There's really nothing wrong with having a bath once in a while, you know,' said Willow in her kindest voice. 'You don't have to be dirty *all* the time.'

'I *like* bein' dirty,' G-Bob argued.

'Me likes beans dirty too!' Ollie agreed, licking his lips. 'Dirty beans, yum!'

'Think about the itch,' Willow said to G-Bob, nodding towards his foot, which he was still clutching in both hands. 'A nice bath will get rid of that for you. You'd like that, wouldn't you?'

G-Bob nodded slowly. His eyes flicked from his foot to the bath and back again.

'Fine,' he mumbled through gritted teeth. 'Fine, then. I'll 'ave a stupid bath. But you ain't gettin' me to take my clothes off!'

The thought of G-Bob getting into the bath with his clothes on was so funny that Pete let out a loud snort of laughter. He quickly clamped his hands over his mouth, but it was too late. G-Bob whipped round and glared at him.

GUSH!

81

'What are you laughin' at?' G-Bob bellowed. 'I'm not 'avin' a bath with you laughin' at me! I'll never 'ave a bath again. Never!'

With that, he pushed past Pete and Ollie and thundered down the stairs like a hairy rhinoceros.

'Oh no!' Pete whispered to Binko.

'Urglegunk,' Binko agreed. 'This is *not* good.'

'Him never barf again,' declared Ollie, crossing his arms. 'No way.'

'Oh well,' Willow sighed, shrugging. 'Maybe next year.'

CHAPTER FIVE

THE SHED

'We need to think of another way to get hold of the chimple,' Binko said as he and Pete followed G-Bob down the stairs, out of the kitchen, past the murky pond and all the way to the bottom of the garden. There stood G-Bob's rotting shed. Propped up on one side by bricks and on the other by an old compost heap, it had a large, cracked, dirty window and a bent chimney with a huge birds' nest in it.

G-Bob spent most of his time locked away in the shed. When he wasn't sleeping, he was snoozing. When he wasn't snoozing, he was napping. And when he wasn't napping, he was *always* grumpy.

Pete knew the shed was off-limits. G-Bob always said if he caught anyone sneaking around in it he'd hang them up by their shoelaces until their heads dropped off. Pete wasn't sure if he believed G-Bob, but the smell of the place alone was enough to keep any sensible person away. Some days the shed smelled like sour milk. Other days it smelled like eggy farts, or rotten vegetables, or sweaty socks.

But today was different – Pete and Binko were on a mission, and nothing was going to stop them. Rolling up his sleeves, Pete grabbed a clothes peg from the washing line and fixed it on his nose as he tiptoed down the path towards the dirty wooden hut.

'Wowzer, that looks zooper,' Binko giggled.

'You won't be laughing when you

smell it,' Pete said, his voice sounding muffled.

As Pete crept up to the shed he could hear G-Bob muttering and moaning inside. Then the smell of the old man's home hit them like a huge stinky truck. Pete's nose was blocked by the peg, but Binko started gasping and stuffing bits of Pete's hair into his tiny nostrils.

'Told you!' Pete whispered smugly.

Binko finally put his helmet on and breathed in deeply. '**FLAMPERING PUFFLEFARTS!**' he gasped. 'That was the worst thing I've ever smelled! And I've smelled a pantpiper's bottom burps!'

Pete slowly raised himself up to the small, dirty window and peeked through.

Strange gizmos filled most of the space inside the shed. They hung from the ceiling and dangled from the walls. Pete couldn't even begin to imagine what most of them actually did.

G-Bob had taken up hundreds of odd hobbies when he wasn't snoozing, but none of them lasted longer than a week. Three weeks ago it was making model planes from custard and matchsticks. Two weeks ago it was 'Bogey Darts'. Last week it was juggling mouldy melons. This week it looked like he was making cheese.

Smelly, *horrible* cheese.

At one end of the shed stood a large metal cauldron filled with runny, mustard-yellow gloop. Every few seconds, a bright-red sink plunger would drop down from

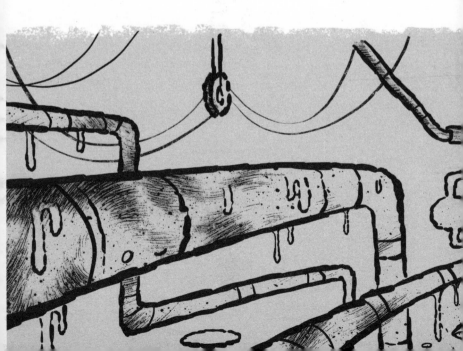

the ceiling on a spring and vanish into the pot, only to pop up with a *shlop* a moment later. Every time the plunger came out, it splattered cheesy gunge over everything in the shed. Including G-Bob.

But the old man didn't seem to notice. He had his foot pressed against a wall and was jabbing under his toenail with a rusty screwdriver, still desperately trying to stop the itch.

'Right,' whispered Binko. 'We need a plan.'

Pete's gaze fell on a crack at the top of the window. A wide smile spread across his face.

'I know,' he said. 'You can use your jet-pack to get through that crack.'

'Oh yeah? And then what?' asked Binko, peering up at the opening.

'Grab the chimple and then jet-pack out. Simple.'

'That's the plan?' squeaked Binko. 'How am I going to get the chimple without being caught? G-Bob'll see me and I'll end up with a rumyet in my drungle!'

Pete looked at G-Bob through the window. He was still rooting around under his nail, this time with an old fishing hook. Every so often Pete caught sight of one of the chimple's long arms coming out from the toenail and making rude gestures with its fingers. G-Bob was itching too much to notice.

'You're just going to have to try,' Pete said. 'I'll think of something that will distract him.'

'Like what exactly?' asked Binko. He looked suspiciously at Pete.

'Um . . .' Pete replied. 'I don't know yet. But I'll think of something.'

Binko sighed. 'All right, I'll give it a go,' he said, revving up his jet-pack. But something was wrong. The jet-pack just rumbled weakly and then stopped.

There was silence for a while, then . . .

'FAT SWANGLING ZUMP-GUZZLERS OF ALPHA CENTAURI!'

Binko bellowed.

'Ouch! No need to shout,' said Pete, covering his ear.

'We've got a problem. My jet-pack's out of fuel.'

'Pants!' muttered Pete. He stared up

at the window for a second, thinking hard.

Then he had an idea.

'I know,' he said, pulling a piece of string out of his pocket. 'I'll lower you down on this.'

'Hm. Are you sure?' replied Binko. He frowned.

'Of course,' said Pete. 'It'll be fun!'

'OK then,' Binko said bravely. Taking hold of the string, he carefully climbed through the crack in the window and Pete slowly lowered him down.

Binko's eyes widened as the toxic air seeped through his helmet. He glared at Pete back through the glass.

'Fun?' he mouthed crossly. 'You call this fun?'

'Don't be such a baby,' Pete mouthed back. 'UGHLEBOOGLE

BLAAAAAA AAAAAAAH!'

yelled G-Bob suddenly. Pete held his breath. It looked like the itching had just got even worse. G-Bob staggered around the shed, waving his arms wildly. One hand knocked into a shelf and sent cheese-making supplies flying in every direction. Then his other hand hit the string that Binko was dangling from. The little alien was flicked up towards the ceiling, flying high above the pot and crashing into loads of hanging metal spoons. Pete gasped as he watched Binko try to cling on to the jingling, swinging spoons. Binko's eyes bulged and his hands clawed at the cutlery.

Then *slooowly* he began to f${}_a$${}_l$${}_l$... **t**u m
b
l
i
n
g
d
o
w
n

. . . right towards G-Bob's vat of cheese!

Thick, slimy cheese sloshed everywhere as Binko hit the surface, sending a shower of dirty yellow droplets over the hooks, ladles and strings of garlic hanging from the shed's ceiling. In an instant the alien had disappeared into the depths of the sticky gloop . . .

CHAPTER SIX
SPLASHDOWN

Pete gasped in horror, his eyes fixed on the cauldron of runny cheese. There was no sign of Binko – only a few ripples, gently spreading out across the surface.

'Come on,' muttered Pete. 'Come on,

Binko, where are you!'

For a few long seconds nothing happened. G-Bob was still jabbing at his toe with a garden rake. Bits of cheese fell gently from the roof like yellow rain.

Then, slowly, a bubble rose to the surface and burst with a pop, revealing Binko's face.

'Result!' Pete whooped with delight. His friend was alive!

His green face looking even greener than usual, Binko swam to the edge of the vat and pulled himself on to the side. Pete punched the air with excitement. Now all they had to do was find a way to get hold of the chimple and all their problems would be over.

Then Pete realised that he wasn't the

only person looking at the cheese-covered little alien. G-Bob was staring at him too.

'AAAARGH!' screamed G-Bob, his eyes bulging. 'It's alive! The cheese is alive!'

Whimpering and yelling, G-Bob turned and threw himself towards the door. With a loud crack, it tore off its hinges and G-Bob fell out of the shed. Still clutching his itchy foot, he hopped off towards the garden gate.

Pete knew he had to act fast. If G-Bob

got away, they could lose the chimple for

good. He had to stop him!

Pete ran and dived towards G-Bob, throwing his arms around his leg.

'Gerroff me!' boomed G-Bob. 'The bliggerin' cheese! It's alive!'

G-Bob was still trying to get away, but with Pete clinging on to his hopping leg, he couldn't keep his balance. With a wail, he tumbled over, taking Pete with him – straight into the garden pond!

The shallow water was icy cold. Pete

opened his mouth to gasp, but a mouthful

of thick, slimy pondwater ran down his

throat. It tasted like cabbage soup after someone had washed their socks in it, and he spat it out as quickly as he could.

'ARGH! Water!' screamed G-Bob. 'I can't stand it! Let me up!'

Suddenly, Pete had an idea. Binko had said that chimples hated getting wet, hadn't he? Maybe the pondwater would force the chimple out!

Grabbing G-Bob's foot, Pete shoved

it under the water.

'Gerroff!' howled G-Bob. 'What the 'eck are you doing?'

There was a flash of movement, and Pete saw Binko flying across the grass, before shooting into the water like a torpedo.

'I'll gut yer gizzards!' cried G-Bob. 'I'll toast yer nose! I'll pickle yer bum!'

But it was no use. Pete held on tightly

117

as Binko swam up to G-Bob's foot, plunged his entire arm under the big toenail and tugged out a long, hairy leg.

'Pull!' shouted Pete.

'GERRROFFF!' screamed G-Bob.

'Eeeeee!' squealed the chimple, as it was pulled out from under G-Bob's toenail with a horrible squelchy sound.

'Gotcha!' cried Binko. Wrapping his arms tightly around the ickimal, he jumped

119

off G-Bob's toe, dragging the struggling chimple behind him.

Pete let go of G-Bob's leg, quickly scooped up Binko and the chimple, one in each hand, and hid them behind his back. With a blast of his jet-pack, Binko was back to his usual place by Pete's ear. Pete kept the other fist closed tightly even though the chimple was gnawing at his fingers.

'Wowzer!' Binko whispered into Pete's

ear. 'G-Bob's stinky cheese came in handy after all – it got my jet-pack working again. It's even more powerful than Pokian fuel!'

G-Bob sat up in the pond, coughing and spluttering, with a large frog on his head.

'Ouch!' Pete exclaimed, as the chimple nibbled at his palm. 'Err, I mean sorry about that,' he said to G-Bob. 'I must have slipped.'

But G-Bob wasn't listening. He was staring down at his toe in amazement.

'It's gone!' he said, splashing around joyfully and throwing pond weed up in the air. 'The itch is bloomin' well gone!'

Pete smiled. 'Well, Mum did tell you that a bath would help,' he said. 'At least this one didn't have bubbles in it . . .'

CHAPTER SEVEN
THAT BATH AGAIN

Back up in his bedroom, Pete tied the chimple up with a piece of string. It sat on his bedside table, growling and gnashing its pointy teeth. Pete couldn't help noticing it looked much fatter than it had before it

 vanished beneath G-Bob's toenail. It had probably eaten enough toe cheese to last it for months.

Binko stood next to it, doing an odd hopping dance.

'Are you OK?' Pete asked him.

'Yes,' Binko panted. 'This is the Pokian foot shuffle of joy.'

Pete tried to copy the funny jumps and turns, but he couldn't keep up. He fell over on his bed with a fit of the giggles. Binko laughed too, and climbed up to sit next to Pete.

'What'll we do with it?' Pete asked, looking at the chimple, who stared back and stuck out a long, toe-cheese-stained tongue.

'What we need,' said Binko, 'is a

Mundolian Plasma Prison with reinforced energy cuffs. Don't suppose you've got one, have you?'

Pete shook his head. Then his eyes gleamed. 'But I do know where there's a vat of stonking cheese that the chimple might like . . .'

Binko jumped up and down on Pete's bed as if it was a trampoline. 'Of course! It's not *toe* cheese, but it'll do. The chimple will live there quite happily until I've found the others and I can take them back to Planet Pok.'

'And G-Bob will never notice,' Pete said. 'He's got a new hobby – the burp pipes! Listen!'

Pete opened his bedroom window so that they could hear the droning burping sound coming from the shed.

'Zooper idea, Pete!' Binko grinned,

giving Pete a tiny high five.

'Thanks.' Pete smiled. 'I guess we make a good team.'

Suddenly, there was a shriek from the door.

'I don't believe it!' cried Willow as she stepped into the room. 'I can't believe what I'm seeing.'

Willow must have spotted Binko!

Pete tried desperately to come up

with an explanation. Maybe he could tell her Binko was a special new robot toy . . . that walked and talked and looked like a tiny alien . . .

'You're such a dirty daisy!' Willow moaned. 'You smell almost as pongy as G-Bob and I didn't think that was *possible*!'

Pete almost laughed with relief.

'Phew,' whispered Binko as he clambered to Pete's ear. 'That was close.'

'There's only one thing for it, my little grime goat,' smiled Willow. 'Bath. Now.'

Pete lay back in the bath, trying to ignore the girly smells that surrounded him. He had pushed out his tummy and was being careful to keep it above the water. Nestled in a pool in Pete's belly button, Binko was having a bath of his own.

131

'So, what next?' asked Pete. 'Where do we find the next ickimal? They won't all be under toenails will they?'

'No,' said Binko. 'Most of them will be in much worse places than that.'

Pete took a deep breath. 'I suppose we'd better start looking for them then.'

'Never fear, Captain Binko and his human sidekick will save the day!' Binko cheered.

'I'm not a sidekick!' Pete laughed, sending a tidal wave over Binko.

'**FLAMPERING PUFFLEFARTS!**' Binko shouted as he was drenched. 'OK, no sidekick. Whatever ickimals we face, however disgusting they may be, *together* we will save the day!'

'That's more like it!' Pete grinned. 'We're the unbeatable Intergalactic Duo!'

THE END

THE CHIMPLE

Prickly black hairs to help it stick under your toenail

Boggly woggly eyes

Sharp, pointy teeth for gobbling up toe cheese

Sticky, stinky toe-cheese dribble

Long droopy arms

Bendy legs for scurrying away quickly